The Brothers G

The Frog Prince

and other fairy tales

Miles Kelly

First published in 2015 by Miles Kelly Publishing Ltd
Harding's Barn, Bardfield End Green, Thaxted, Essex, CM6 3PX, UK

2 4 6 8 10 9 7 5 3 1

Publishing Director Belinda Gallagher
Creative Director Jo Cowan
Editorial Director Rosie Neave
Designer Rob Hale
Production Manager Elizabeth Collins
Reprographics Stephan Davis, Jennifer Cozens, Thom Allaway

ISBN 978-1-78209-741-9

Printed in China

British Library Cataloguing-in-Publication Data
A catalogue record for this book is available from the British Library

ACKNOWLEDGEMENTS
The publishers would like to thank the following artists who have contributed to this book:

Front cover and all border illustrations: Louise Ellis (The Bright Agency)

Inside illustrations:
The Frog Prince Mónica Carretero (Plum Pudding Illustration Agency)
The Fisherman and His Wife Claudia Venturini (Plum Pudding Illustration Agency)
The Queen Bee Kristina Swarner (The Bright Agency)
The Spindle, the Shuttle and the Needle Ayesha Lopez (The Bright Agency)

Made with paper from a sustainable forest

www.mileskelly.net
info@mileskelly.net

Contents

The Frog Prince

Long ago, there lived a king who had three daughters. The young women were all lovely, and many princes came to seek their hands in marriage. But everyone agreed that the youngest princess was loveliest of all.

4

Near the royal family's castle, there was a shady wood. In summer, the youngest princess liked nothing better than to walk through the wood to a well. There she would stay, playing with a golden ball she often carried, admiring it in the dappled light.

One hot day, the princess was doing just that when her ball suddenly slipped through her fingers. It hit the ground and bounced up over the edge of the well, dropping into the water with a splash. The princess peered down inside the well, but she could see nothing but darkness. She sank down onto the mossy ground and started to cry.

"Don't upset yourself," said a croaky voice. "I can get your ball back."

The princess looked up, startled. There was no one around except for a plump frog squatting on the edge of the well. "Really?" she gasped, brightening.

"Yes, of course," reassured the frog. "But what will you give me, if I do?"

"Oh, *anything*," gushed the delighted girl. "My silver shoes… my golden purse… even my diamond tiara!"

"No, no," gulped the frog, "what would I do with those? Just promise that we will be best friends." His bulging eyes grew soft. "I want to be with you all day, every day. I want to eat with you off your golden plate, and sleep in your comfy bed. What fun we will have together!"

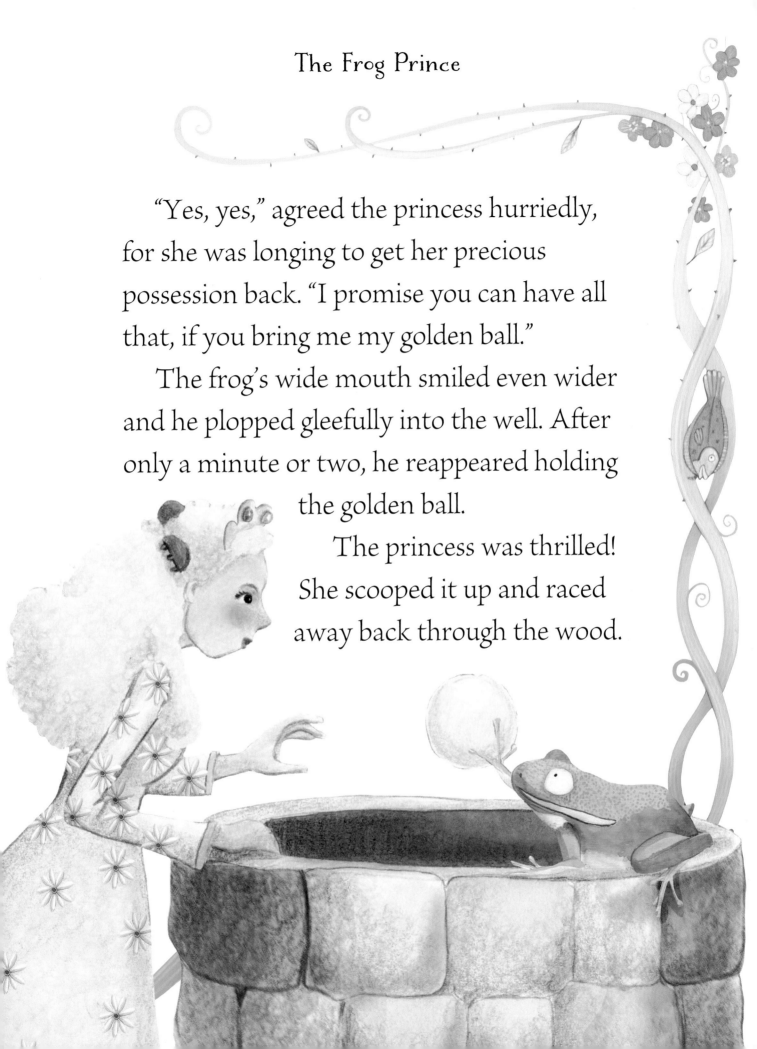

"Yes, yes," agreed the princess hurriedly, for she was longing to get her precious possession back. "I promise you can have all that, if you bring me my golden ball."

The frog's wide mouth smiled even wider and he plopped gleefully into the well. After only a minute or two, he reappeared holding the golden ball.

The princess was thrilled! She scooped it up and raced away back through the wood.

"Wait! Wait!" called the frog, leaping after her. "Pick me up! I cannot go as fast as you!"

But in her joy, the king's daughter had forgotten all about her helper. She dashed on home to the castle and the poor frog was left far behind.

That evening, when the princess and the king were eating dinner, there came a noise of something flopping wetly up the castle's staircase – *splish, splash, splish, splash!* Then there was a knocking at the door of the great hall and a voice cried, "Youngest princess, please let me in!"

Curious, the princess went to see who it could be. But when she opened the door and saw the frog sitting there, she slammed it shut at once. Horrified, she sat back down without saying a word.

The king noticed that his daughter was trembling and asked, "Whatever has frightened you? Has a giant come to carry you away?" and he chuckled fondly.

But the princess grew pale. "It's no giant," she said, in a very small voice. "It's a horrid frog." And she explained what had happened the day before.

Then the knocking began again and the frog's voice said: "Youngest princess, let me in! I want what you promised me!"

The king looked grave. "You made a promise and you must keep it," he said firmly.

The youngest princess stood slowly, took a

deep breath, and went to let the frog in.

The frog hopped at her heels back to her chair. "Lift me up so I can sit with you," he croaked. The princess turned away in disgust, but the king insisted that she do as the frog had asked.

Once the frog was on the table next to the princess, he said, "Now push those golden plates a little nearer, so that we may eat together."

And the princess had to obey.

When the frog's tummy was full, he gave a yawn.

"Delicious," he said, "but now I'm tired. Let's go to bed."

Then the princess hung her head and began to weep. But the king gave her a stern look. So she picked up the slimy creature with just her finger and thumb, and held him out away from her. She carried him upstairs to her bedroom and dropped him in a corner, before quickly jumping into bed and drawing the covers over her head.

Then the frog came hopping up to her bedside, croaking, "Let me snuggle in too, or I will tell your father."

The princess groaned. She threw back the quilt and let the frog leap onto the mattress alongside her. But at the touch of his cold, damp skin she grew angry. "That's enough!" she yelled, and she seized the frog and tossed him away.

As he fell, something very strange happened. The frog began to blur and change and grow. And then, to the princess's astonishment, a handsome prince with the kindest face she had ever seen was suddenly standing in front of her. The prince smiled and gently explained how a wicked witch had enchanted him. The princess was the only one who could save him and, by carrying out her promise, she had broken the spell.

The prince knelt before the princess in thanks and, as they gazed into each other's eyes, they fell deeply in love.

Of course, the king was delighted and gave his permission for the joyful couple to get married. And it wasn't long before they set off to the prince's kingdom in a golden carriage drawn by eight white horses, with crowds of well-wishers cheering them along the way.

The Fisherman and His Wife

Once upon a time, there was a poor fisherman who lived with his wife in a shack by the sea. Every morning the fisherman went out fishing, and every evening he returned with only one or two

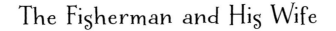

little fish – just enough food to keep them from starving.

One day, the fisherman was astonished to pull up his line and see a huge flounder dangling from it.

"Hey, fisherman!" the big fish said. "I beg you, let me live. I'm not really a flounder – I'm an enchanted prince! Please let me go."

"Of course," agreed the fisherman. He put the flounder back into the water so it could swim away and he hurried home.

"Have you caught nothing at all today?" grumbled his wife.

"Not exactly," said the man. "I caught a talking flounder who said he was an enchanted prince, can you believe? He asked me to let him go so of course I did."

"Didn't you wish for anything first?" moaned the woman.

"No," said the man. "It didn't cross my mind. What could I have wished for?"

"Well, look around," sighed the woman, "it's awful to live in this shack. You might have wished for a small cottage. Go and find the flounder and ask him."

The man didn't feel comfortable about it, but his wife moaned and moaned until at last he gave in and went back to the sea. The water was no longer clear but grey and choppy as he called out:

"Flounder, flounder in the sea,
 Come, I beg you, here to me."

Then the flounder came swimming up to him and said, "Well, what do you want?"

"It's not me," said the man, "it's my wife. She does not want to live in a shack any longer. She would like a cottage."

"Go, then," said the flounder, "she has it already."

17

When the man went home, his wife was no longer in the shack, but in a little cottage. There was a porch, and pretty rooms filled with lovely furniture. Behind the cottage was a garden with hens and flowers and fruit. "Look," said the wife, "isn't this nice?"

The couple lived happily for about a fortnight, until the woman announced, "Listen, husband, I want to live in a castle. Go to the flounder and ask for one." And she moaned and moaned until at last the fisherman went back to the sea.

The sky was heavy and the waves were churning as the fisherman called out:

"Flounder, flounder in the sea,
   Come, I beg you, here to me."

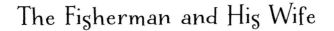

Then the flounder appeared out of the surf and said, "Well, what does your wife want now?"

"Alas," said the fisherman, feeling rather scared, "she wants to live in a castle."

"Go then, she has it," said the flounder.

Then the man went home. But instead of the cottage he found a massive stone castle. There was a great hall with servants. There were beautiful wall hangings and thick carpet. A crystal chandelier hung from the ceiling over a huge stone table laid with fine food and wine. Behind the castle there was a courtyard with stables and horses, and a magnificent park beyond.

"Look at it all!" said his wife. "Isn't this

beautiful?" And they enjoyed a feast and went to bed.

Next morning the wife prodded her husband awake and said, "Get up. I want to be king over all the land! Go to the flounder and ask him." And she moaned and moaned until at last the man went back to the sea, muttering, "It is not right…" all the way.

When he came to the sea, the sky was pitch-black. A strong wind whipped up enormous waves as the fisherman called:

"Flounder, flounder in the sea,

Come, I beg you, here to me."

The flounder heard him and came to the shore and said, "Well, what does your wife want this time?"

"Alas," said the fisherman, "she wants to be king now."

"Go then," replied the flounder. "She is king already."

When the fisherman came to where the castle had been he saw a gleaming palace. Ranks of soldiers stood outside and, as he approached, they threw open the enormous doors. There were splendid courtiers in a magnificent hall, and his wife was sitting on a huge silver throne, wearing a golden crown on her head.

"Husband," the fisherman's wife announced. "I know I am now the king and can rule over people… but I want to be able to order the moon to rise and the sun to set –

I want to be God."

"No," said the exasperated fisherman, "I cannot ask that of the fish."

His wife grew very angry. "What!" she cried. "I am the king, and you are nothing but my husband. I order you to go and ask this instant!"

Then the fisherman was afraid, but he had to go. A great storm was raging as he stood by the sea and called:

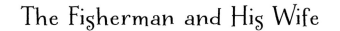

"Flounder, flounder in the sea,
Come, I beg you, here to me."

Then the flounder rose from the crashing waves and said, "Well, what can your wife want for now?"

"Alas," whispered the fisherman, quaking, "she wants to be God."

"Go then," said the flounder, "and you will find her back again in the shack."

And there they are both still living to this very day.

The Queen Bee

Once upon a time there was a king who had three sons. When the two eldest princes grew up, they each went off into the world to seek adventures. But they both made one mistake after another, and fell in with bad people and wasted their money, so they never made it home. The youngest prince, whom everyone called Prince Nitwit, really missed his brothers. So when he was old enough, he set off to join them.

Prince Nitwit had to work hard to find his brothers. To his surprise, when he found them at last, the two eldest princes weren't pleased to see him. "So you've tracked us down so you can have adventures too, have you?" they jeered. "Well, we're brainy and brave and we've made a mess of things, so what on earth makes you think that a simpleton like you is going to be a hero?" But eventually, after a good deal of complaining, Prince Nitwit's big brothers said they would let him travel along with them.

The three hadn't gone far when they came to an ant-hill. The two eldest princes had a nasty idea – to stir up the ant-hill with a stick, so they could laugh at the tiny insects scurrying off in terror. But Prince Nitwit wouldn't hear of it. "Leave them alone," he said. "I won't let you hurt them." His brothers grumbled about it, but at last they agreed to travel on.

They soon came to a lake where ducks were swimming. The two eldest princes discussed how they could kill some and eat them. But Prince Nitwit forbade it. "No way," he said. "We already have enough food to eat." His brothers complained about it, but eventually they agreed to travel on.

Soon they spotted a bees' nest in a tree, overflowing with honey. The two eldest princes wanted to make a fire underneath the tree to smoke the bees out, so they could steal the honey. But Prince Nitwit would not hear of it. "Absolutely not," he said. His brothers sneered at him, but finally agreed to travel on.

One morning, the three princes came to a towering castle – but there was no sign of any people or animals anywhere. They crossed the silent drawbridge and passed the stables – all totally bare. Nervously, the princes entered the keep. Every room was furnished, just as if people were living there, but there wasn't a soul in sight!

Through empty room after empty room the princes crept, until they wandered into a huge hall where there was a stone table. The princes saw that there was some unusual writing on it. Prince Nitwit realized what it was at once. "It's instructions telling us how to release this castle from its enchantment!" he gasped, and he read aloud to his brothers what they had to do (for they weren't as good at reading as he was).

"In the wood under some moss lie one thousand pearls belonging to a princess. Find them by sunset – but if even one is missing, you will be turned into stone. Next—"

The Queen Bee

"Pah! That sounds easy enough," interrupted the eldest prince. "Leave it to me." He set off into the wood. But though he searched high and low all day, at the end of it he had found only one hundred pearls. At sunset, the last sunbeam soaked into the land, and he was turned to stone.

The second brother was determined to prove that he was braver, brainier and better than the eldest. The next day, he set off into the forest to take his turn. But alas, he did only slightly better. By sunset he had found just two hundred of the gleaming pearls and he too was turned to stone.

Poor Prince Nitwit was on his own again once more. On the morning of the third day, he set out to complete the task that his brothers had failed at, but he felt so miserable about his brothers that he hadn't found many pearls at all before he sat down and began to weep.

Suddenly, *march, march, march*! Up came the king of the ant-hill that Prince Nitwit had saved, with five thousand ant soldiers. It wasn't long at all before the little insects had collected all one thousand of the pearls and put them in a heap.

Prince Nitwit's heart lifted. He thanked the ants heartily and then hurried to read the next instruction on the table:

Fetch the key of the princesses'
sleeping-chamber out of the lake.

Prince Nitwit went and looked at the huge mirror-like expanse of water in dismay. He knew it would take him years to find the key hidden in the murky depths. But just then the two ducks whose lives he had saved came

swimming up. They upped tails and dived down to the bottom of the lake, and came up, one carrying the lost key in its beak!

Prince Nitwit was overjoyed and thanked the ducks heartily. Now all he had to do was follow the final instruction, which he now read:

Choose the youngest and loveliest of the three sleeping princesses.

But this was a truly impossible task! Prince Nitwit found the room where the three princesses lay sleeping, but they all looked equally beautiful, and each appeared to be just as young as the other! As Prince Nitwit stood there, about to despair, the Queen bee of the bees' nest that he had saved came buzzing along. The clever Queen bee remembered that before the youngest princess had been enchanted, she had eaten a spoonful of honey. She landed on the lips of each princess one by one and hovered over the one where she tasted honey.

And so it was, that Prince Nitwit made the right choice and broke the spell. The three princesses woke up and the two stone statues in the woods were changed back into Prince Nitwit's brothers. Of course, Prince Nitwit married the youngest, loveliest princess and became king, and his brothers married the other two princesses.

And that's how, thanks to the Queen bee, Prince Nitwit became the hero of a truly amazing adventure.

The Spindle, the Shuttle and the Needle

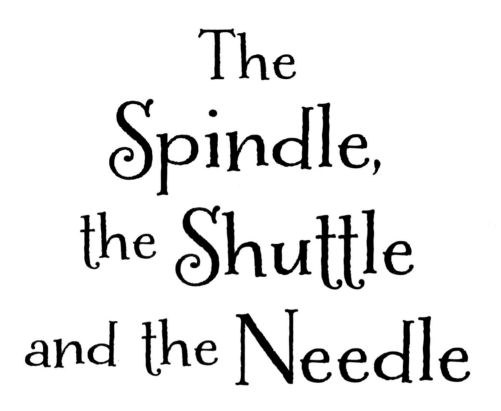

There was once a little girl whose parents died. She went to live with her grandmother, who earned a living by spinning, weaving and sewing. The old woman brought up the girl to be good, kind and hard-working. But when the girl was just grown up, the old woman fell very ill. She said to the girl, "I want you to have my house, so you always have a place to live, and my spindle, shuttle and needle, so you can always earn a living." Then the old lady died.

So the girl lived in the little house, all alone, and was able to live on the money she made by spinning, weaving and sewing.

About this time, the son of the king went travelling around the country looking for a bride. He told everyone, "I shall marry the girl who is the poorest and the richest, at the same time." No one knew what that meant, but they did know it meant he was looking for someone very special.

One day, the prince passed through the girl's village. He stopped his horse and peered in through her window. There the girl sat at her spinning wheel, busily working. When she saw the prince, she blushed and cast her eyes down, and worked faster than ever.

After the prince had rode on, one of the girl's grandmother's sayings came to her lips: "Spindle, my spindle, hurry away, and here to my house bring my sweetheart, I pray."

The spindle sprang out of her hand and out of the door, and skipped merrily away down the road, trailing a bright, shining blue thread after it. As the girl now had no spindle, she took the weaver's shuttle in her hand and began to weave at her loom.

Meanwhile, the spindle danced on, and it reached the prince. "Whatever have we here?" he cried. "This spindle wants me to follow it!" He turned his horse around and rode back, following the shining thread towards the girl's home.

There she sat at her loom, singing: "Shuttle, my shuttle, weave well this day, and guide my sweetheart to me here, I pray." At once the shuttle sprang out of her hand and leapt out of the door. It began to weave the most

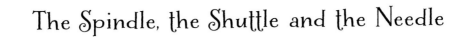

beautiful carpet she had ever seen.

Next, the girl sat down to sew. She held the needle in her hand and sang: "Needle, my needle, sharp-pointed and fine, prepare this house for a sweetheart of mine."

Then the needle leapt out of her fingers and flew about the room. It covered tables with damask tablecloths, and chairs with velvet cushions, and hung silk curtains at the windows.

The needle had just put in the last stitch when the girl

saw the prince coming, following the shining thread. He got down from his horse and stepped over the amazing carpet into the beautifully decorated house. There stood the poor girl, but she was so lovely that she shone like a rose surrounded by leaves.

"You are truly the poorest and the richest girl," the prince said, taking her hand. "You will be my bride." The wedding was held at the castle with much rejoicing. The spindle, shuttle and needle were put in the treasure chamber for safe-keeping – and you can see them there still.